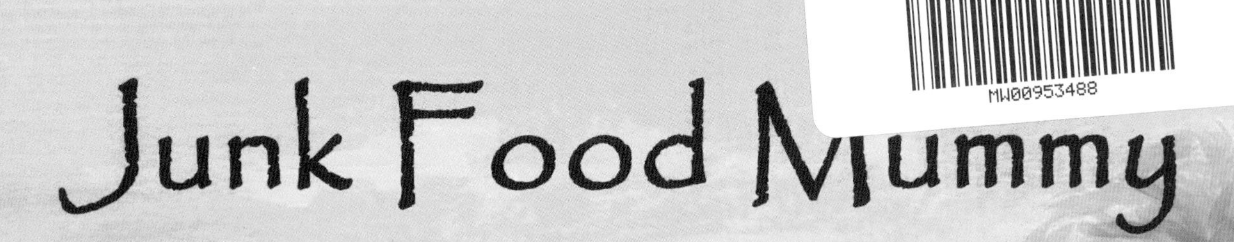

Junk Food Mummy

by Mary Ruth Hughes
illustrated by DiAne H. Gillespie
and Roger A. Gillespie

Junk Food Mummy

Library of Congress-in-Cataloging-in-Publication Data

Willow Vista Books
www.WillowVistaBooks.com
Printed in the United States of America

SECOND EDITION

2012

Juvenile Fiction

ISBN-10: 1478141379 ISBN-13: 978-1478141372

There once was a
mummy that had a
skinny little tummy
and he lived in the
bottom of a tomb
The years he was
there that pyramid
was bare he was
hoping for a meal
real soon

He saw a
light
thought what
a sight
must lie beyond
my jail

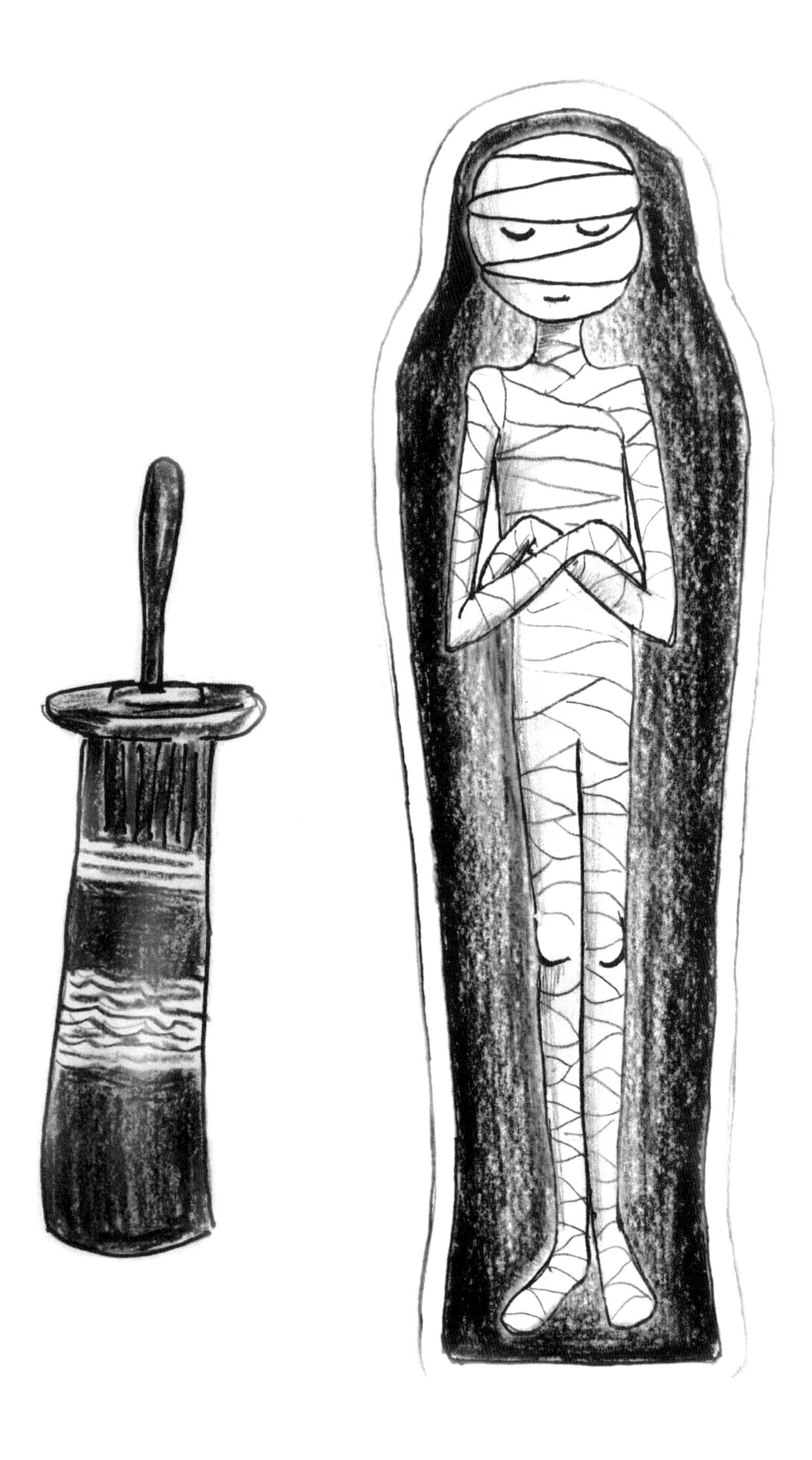
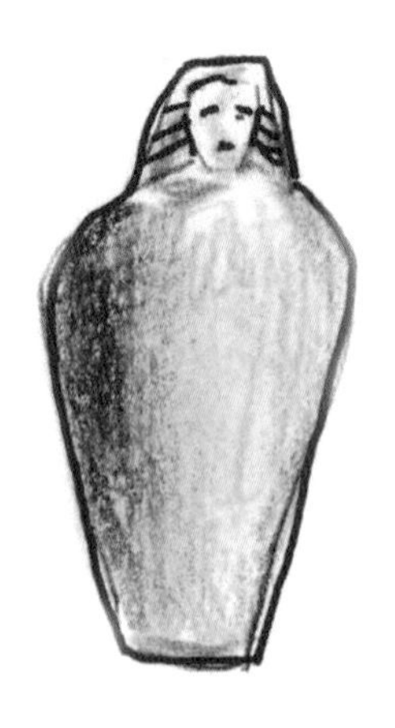
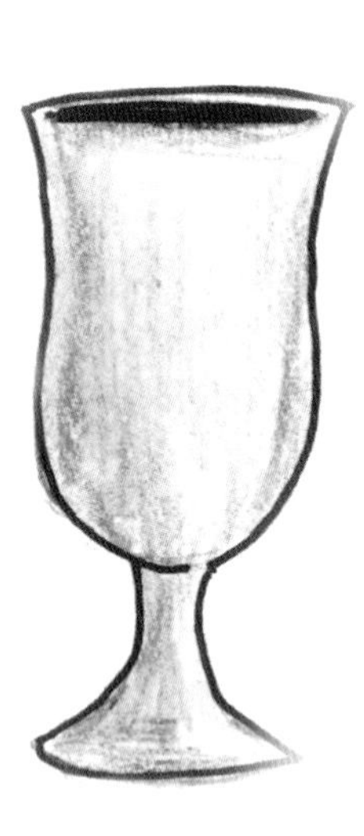

This
sarcophagus
must come
off a-muss
that's when
he made a
plan to leave
his cell

Tummy Gauge
empty
full
GRRR...

Yum yum yummy
a growling tummy
hunger pains from
a starving mummy

Through the tunnel
like a funnel
aromas kept pushing
him on
burgers fries
and cherry pies
and hot dogs
one foot long

alley of the Kings
burgers fries
The Red Sea
sodas
RED SEA SODA

As time went by
he ate more
and more pie
bigger and bigger
he grew

His mummy
wraps became
little straps
and right off
of him they flew

Yum yum yummy
he filled his tummy
and now he's a
junk food
junkie mummy
(repeat)

His great big belly
would shake like jelly
he was a giant
mummy king
he couldn't wait
so he ate and ate
all the kids
began to sing

Pizza with cheese
hold the anchovies
please he's a whole
lot bigger than me
blimp in size with
thunder thighs now
he's wearing a
string bikini

Junk Food Mummy

Chorus
F# C Em Am E7
Yum Yum Mum-my a growl-ing tum-my Hun-ger pains from a

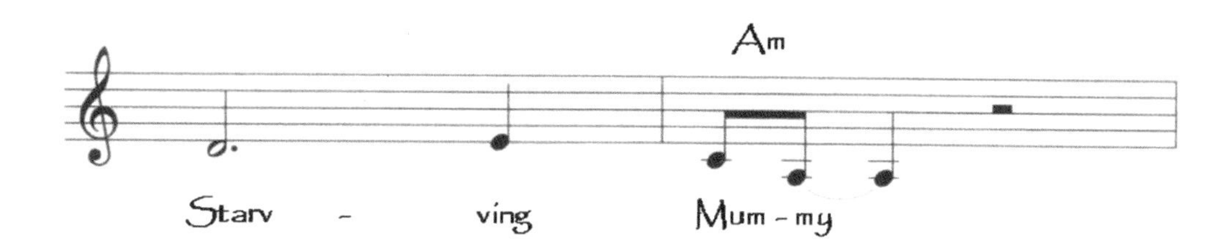
Am
Starv - ving Mum - my

Chorus 2

Yum Yum Yummy
He filled his tummy
And now he's a junk Food
Junky ....Mummy.

WillowVistaBooks.com

The Old Toad
by Mary Ruth Hughes
illustrated by DiAne H. Gillespie
Roger A. Gillespie

Junk Food Mummy
by Mary Ruth Hughes
illustrated by DiAne H. Gillespie
and Roger A. Gillespie

Ghost Dancin'
Zydeco

MONSTERS
BY MARY RUTH HUGHES
ILLUSTRATED BY DIANE H GILLESPIE
AND ROGER A. GILLESPIE

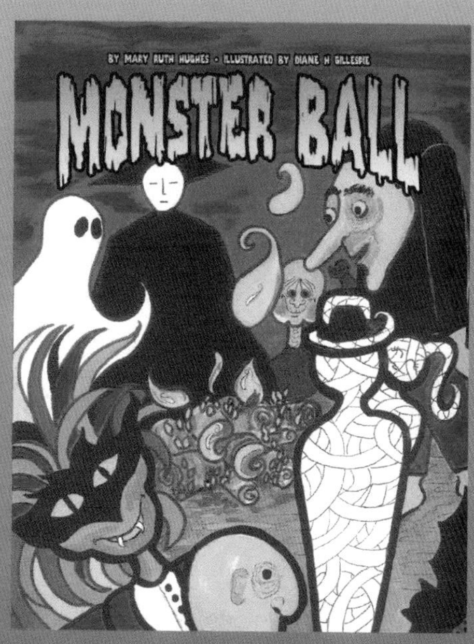
BY MARY RUTH HUGHES · ILLUSTRATED BY DIANE H GILLESPIE
MONSTER BALL

CREATURES
by Mary Ruth Hughes
illustrated by DiAne H. Gillespie

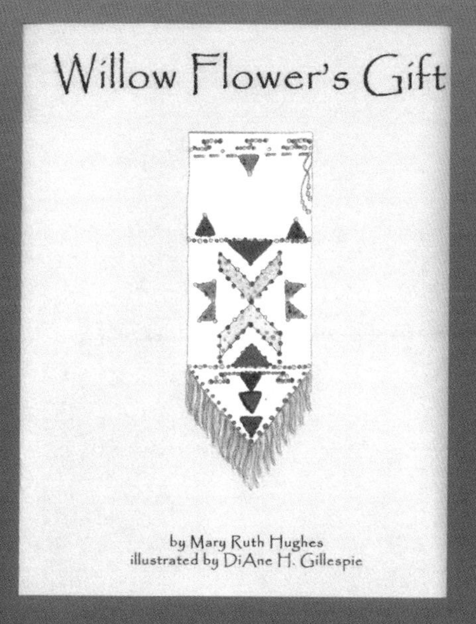
Willow Flower's Gift
by Mary Ruth Hughes
illustrated by DiAne H. Gillespie

Mary Ruth Hughes
Tishomingo

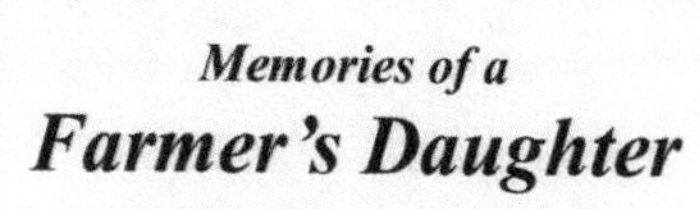
Memories of a
Farmer's Daughter

by Jennie Phelps

Made in the USA
San Bernardino, CA
21 February 2014